Parameter of Life

Yeshi Gemaneh

PublishAmerica
Baltimore

Hardcover 978-1-4489-7812-0
Softcover 978-1-4489-6510-6
PUBLISHED BY PUBLISHAMERICA, LLLP
www.publishamerica.com
Baltimore

Printed in the United States of America

INTRODUCTIION

Poetry, you polished my thinking
Changed my view point
Expressed my feelings beyond the horizon
Anger, joy, or value
You gave me a chance to burst out
I learned and refined by appraisal
I know that I am not a poet;
Only a learner: I call them
"My ABC Poems"
My writing is not private
But to share with many
To make a pitch into the Ocean
Don't call me a poet; I am still a learner

Yeshi Gemaneh

My Childhood Friend

A memory brought so much
The joy we shared
We were rich in toys
And products of nature

The mud and rock with both hands
Listening to stories under a tree
Were equally enjoyable then
That is a bond if I may call it

Playing hide and seek "Kukululu"
The places we went
Jumping into a pond
The entire frolic I remember

We looked in all directions
To pick unripe mangoes
To hide wrong-doing
We swore on all saints

Keeping her head down
Mama running to shout
A lot more to share
My childhood friend

Education

The menu I most love
Life saving scent I breathe
When curtains of illiteracy torn down
To see the delightful light
Help polish the wrong outlook
Much more to glance on the darker part
A father of wisdom a flush light of life
Vision too short without you
Offer your menu to all
Everyone needs you
Understanding ambivalent
without you
You are with big value in life
Education

This is Today

This is a season where leaves fly
Sun and cloud try evenly share space
All kind of people walk on the street
Jogger's brick around the lake
Elderly struggle with their walkers
Sit at a wooden bench stared at each other
No common language to converse
The birds flocking common entertainers
Rose of Sharon en route for many
I sneak through the window from my studio
How did I arrive here, who knows?
Anyway, life is like a shadow
With gratitude for years behind

Good Old Time

The meadow wide and level
Where the herds graze
Plenty space for kids as well
Ridding on horse back
From village to town
Greeted each other
As if they knew for years
Children scattered everywhere
Shouted and chanted
Run to chase each other
In between stopped
For friendly gesture
To passer by
In return received elderly blessing
Kids so dear in the neighborhood
The sun watching every step
That is what I called Day of My Time

Ethiopia

To those who remember
Surging back to the golden age
Rich black soil yielded two crops a year
Considerable water flowed over the dam
All the fruit that grew in the East
All the corn that grew in the West
The original Coffee that grew in Keffa
Once you were called, "A Land of Basketful of Bread."
All the good news piled up changed to:
Famine, war, and hunger
Oh, you, torn apart by man and nature
Now your legacy speaks to my grandchild
Nothing but hunger
Appeal to the world to save a dying child

You and Me

One might think this is a hard hit
There are many more worst than you think
Think less fortunate ones
When health gets jeopardized
Sudden death of loved one's
When a child loose parent at early age
When one remain on the way
Before the hair turning grey
When one faces with insolvent puzzles
When no bread on the table
Digging garbage in search of food
A heart that never broken will never
Know the others pain
A word of gratitude: for the air we breathe
For the sunshine to worm up our cold body
They too human like you and me

Let Us Play

Let us play "Qelebosh"
My childhood game
Which is swinging in my mind?
With years of memory
That game is a treasure to me
With five marbles up and down
Unique to Westerners
A combination of art and skill
Good exercise to hand and mind
To lose or to win part of a game
That was a game taught me to count
To add and subtract
Retreat was out of question
Memory remain vicarage and fresh
At my birth town, Harar
Where is my childhood friend?
I like to play it again

Words of Gratitude

Dressed with double garment
Blessed with wonderful:
Family and friends
Holding me up when I slide
The few nice words uttered
Keep me smile
Delightful hope shining on my face
All the pain in my heart polished
Overpowered by slight touch of love
"It could happen to anyone
Not alone, keep on crawling
You are our big tree
We can shade under you
Weather on rain or burning sun
Keep on walking,"
These are the words ringing in my ears
Thank you my children,
My family and m friends
Above all to My God for His Love

My Birth Land, Ethiopia

On high plateau
On ragged mountain
Surrounded by hills and valley
You scolded of your droughts
With no fault of yours
All your beauty covered by swift
Dust
Your hospitality changed
To second degree begging bread
For hungry
You raised me with milk and honey
Somewhere went wrong
Can you tell me?
You a mother of burnet face
Call them to change your neck-names
I know, you will be blessed again
Now and then always remain my country

Congratulations to Elect-President Obama

I voluntarily picked my broken pen
To utter a few words
This is extra event invite many scholar's
of the world
This time history did not repeat itself
This is a day break with a new chapter
Needs are many listen to heart beat in agony
Make your wisdom as loose as a wind
as deep as an ocean
Let all abundantly collect cordial fruit
You made a loud call to all for change!
With pragmatic promises for fair treatment to all
Undying hope remain forever more
Finally; I bow my head down as a courteous
And Congratulate to "ilmakaacjhaa" Our Son

S

Speak to me say it out loud
Share what you have in your mind
Second hand taught save us from default
Scholastic thinking put us in advance
Summer is always pleasant
Surprise will put us in excitement
Senior years for respect
Swimming help we escape from sinking
Survivals are full of adventure
Social studies help for better understanding
Sound travels a long distance
Scamming is against morality
Sincerity what we all need
Simplicity for better solidarity

Happy New Year

Here and there blanketed with
ye Meskel Abeba
Stunning yellow flower
A God-given present
The sign of the New Year
A heritage celebration --
It is welcomed with songs:
ababayea hoy; lamlem…
A song wishing fertility and green growth
And heartwarming experience
And health and wealth
Full of cheerful blessings
Going from house to house
Maintaining cultural identity
Youngsters present bouquets of flowers
To neighbors and relatives
To fill up all empty spaces with
Love and harmony
And wish for new beginnings
To follow a wise man's journey
To be ready for a new resolution
enqu'ettash bayymetu yamttash
Happy New Year every one!

My Thought

A hidden friend in the jungle
With flush light every now and then
Any time I need, right there
Never put me down
For ever and a day, on summit
Which I am proud of
My lifelong treasure
Nurturing with positive outlook
Will save from decayed
Don't care of others negativity
They tried to sale me
When they have none out there
Always proud of you, My Thought

AFRICA

You the largest and populous
Surrounded by Sea and Lakes
Decorated by rainforest, Valley and Gorge
Unlimited beauty of human history
Blue Nile and Great Rift Valley your entity
Home to wild animals
Your blackness a sign of beauty
Year in, year out they call you poor
They don't try to pull you out
They don't show you know-how
When you have immense wealth to use
Luck of good-will venture blocked the road
Calling you poor is unrealistic
When they share your wealth
Guidance what is essential, not disapproval

The Happy Life

Never again past is gone
The happy life now I find
With no worry of the future
In compacted hazy room
Whatever available asking for His Bless
Pure glass of water cause no pain
No rules that abide me other than my conscious
My peaceful mind is a joy of a day
My good night sleep releases worry
Is there any one there who change
rules of nature?
My gratitude is always present

Thank You!

Yellow, white, black, brown
You host each and all
All can hear your voice from a distance
The ringing bell inside your heart is a triumph
After hard labor you gave birth to democracy
Gathered under your shade in search of
the lost freedom
Stretch your hands up to reach those left out
Let all sing a song of equity
There are still many buried in agony
Browse through your vocabulary for poverty
Open your eyes wide to see the lost
You happen to be an affectionate mother
You offer bread and butter
Thank you, Statue of Liberty!

What is Your Name?

When you could be a designer of your own life
I can feel your silence buried inside
In this frosty cold winter
You remain with sleepless eyes
Shabby, worn-out cloth on top of your head
Supreme darkness alerted on your face
The wind whispering in your ears
Soon, trembling in your chilly nest
With no recovery of hope in this paradise
World
Something went wrong somewhere
I wonder if your case has been taken
To the chamber of the elite
I am a lay person, I cannot offer much advice
If you are a victim of secret habits,
Please stop them now
I can only say my heart is broken in pieces
To see you this way you homeless man.

On the Way to Lunenburg

Feeling an importance I couldn't fill
Blush on my face—smile of happiness
Mother whispered into my ear
"Go learn, and pass it on to the next generation"
I sneezed from a mixed weather: cold and warm
The first word I heard was "Gesundheit"
From what I have learned, it means, "bless you"
What good wishing someone from a strange land?
My eyes were most grateful viewing what
I hadn't seen before
Well-dressed people made me think…
Less fortunate ones of mine
Murmured inside, is this magic?
"No, it is by hard work and education"
Soon, I am in "Bahnhof" train station

I Hope You Would Agree

I hope you would agree
To revoke to purchase a child
To a foreign land
Let him grow in his own village
We need to balance between:
Material and human touch
No matter how poor he is
Should retain dignity and culture
What is important is, "I love you."
Not I will buy you
If anyone in sympathy
Should help a child
While playing with mud and rock
In his own yard
A child is human not a pet
Poverty is not a disease
It is a matter of hard work
And education

Life
Dedication to the September 11, 2001 tragedy

On my first day of birth
I cry bitterly when I taste the
sourness of life
Mom rubs me with foam of love
Dad runs out to consult the stars
Can my horoscope reveal?
Which name would best fit?
None of these will claim
A day will come, life escaping fear,
Pain and sorrow
Leaving the beauty of nature
The sea, the mountain and the ocean behind
No wonder I cried bitterly
Forecasted far more than a real dream
Did the stars tell the truth?

Acceptance

When hardship is on the way
When defeat and rejection overpower
When hope seems to migrate
When life is hard
Acceptance is powerful
Not only success the venue of conversation
Talk also of the failure
Leave behind the superficial material interest
All need reaffirmation of life
Whether victory or defeat
Acceptance is what brings together

Time or Me

I too was innocent
We all gathered in that compacted room
Everyone took turn to tell
Tale of a day
Exploded into laughter
Who would think that time will pass?
It did slowly but surly
Who to be blamed
For unwisely used time

I too was innocent
With fresh thinking
Not far sighted
All that had pass quickly
It really did swept rapidly
Who to be blamed
For the ambushed
Me or time

Now sitting alone
In a room of the same size
Where are all gathered around
Who giggled, and chanted
Full of lives
Non around just alone
Am I imaging
No that is the journey

Good-Bye '99

A year goes and a year comes
This is your turn to say "farewell"
And, through and over everything
This moment is the best the world can offer
And move on with memories as clouds do
A sweet season, oh, beautiful Christmas in you
The wish and the freshness of a dream also
Sparkled
We hear, and learn the damage you've done
Forgiveness is divine
Goodbye to you and welcome, Millennium
With peace and love.

Who Am I?

I carried my baby at the back
I hold fire wood on my front
I walked miles to fetch water
I took lunch for farming husband
I broom the floor in between
I go to farm to help on the weed
No umbrella for burning sun
I munch as I walked; no time for lunch
Dog and cat sneak for crumbs
Rushed to pick egg laid before it crushes
I milk cow in the evening
I nurse my crying baby at night
At worst I hammed out loud
On Sunday, I go to church to pray
For sin inherited from ancestors
I wonder when this would end
They called me a woman of a farm

Self-Portrait

You whom I see in me
From the black soil of Africa
A big family tree
With many branches around you
As you vividly see yourself . . .
You've never been told your memory of
Dusseldorf
From your room, you listened to the flow
Of the Rhine River. . .
Natural light twinkles through a window
Family picture hangs on a wall
A potted plant at the very end
Thinking of the future, reliving the past
Past is history, future is hope
Present is hardship, don't give up . . .
Soon I fall asleep, bidding good night
To that cozy room

Good Hope Village

Yeshi Gemaneh

Good Hope Village
Table of Contents

Introduction

I was born and raised in East Ethiopia, in an ancient, Arabian-nights look city called Harar. I had a wonderful childhood, going back and forth with my parents from Harar to our farm land called *Mollea*. My childhood memories of the countryside and its beautiful landscapes, the densely forest, the herds, the birds and all the crops – barley, corn, wheat, fruit, and vegetables – not to mention the best coffee – still vibrate in my mind.

Later, mothers offer children only dried breasts as a period of misery and despair – horrible famine – came to the region. As I recall the facts of my childhood though, I want to share my memories of the region Harar which I call it "Rainbow Town." And the farm place Mollea, Good Hope Village.

Part One: Good-Hope Village

Wild flowers were cherished around their cottages; such as lily of the valley, bluebell, African violet and foxglove. They grew by accident, not purposely planted. In the thatched roof cottage, burning wood smoke elevated like pillars. There is a little hole on the side of the cottage only for some fresh air to get in.

Rooster crowed, announcing the dawn to the villagers, eliminating their need for a clock tower and contributing to their happiness.

ABabu, the only son of his mother Negate and father Habitu, preferred to play with his mother. ABabu and his mother were so close.

"Emma, let us play," ABabu asked his mother.

"Play?"

"Yes, play."

"I am tired, son" She took a deep breath.

"What is tired?" ABabu asked, surprised.

The villagers had no running water; instead, water was carried in gourds or pots on heads or backs, from a river – near or far. "I have been working the whole day. Don't you see what I have done? I carried the water you poured for *Korea* Dog from the river," she answered, hoping he would understand.

"When I grow up... "ABabu started sneaking through the open space that marked their small door.

"What? "When you grow up…"? Finish it."

ABabu turned to face her. "I will get you everything you need."

"What can you get me, son?" Negate smiled.

"I will dig a well for you and for Good Hope villagers. Also, I will buy all the things you need."

Negate pulled her worn-out sweater around her at the sound of a shout outside. "What is that sound I hear? By the way, where is *Korea* Dog? Go look for him. ABabu. "ABabu scratched his head and looked around, going outside; the room was quiet. He returned with a frog: "Let us play; Emma."

Negate jumped up and down in the tiny room: "Get out of the house! Get out of the house with what you have in your hand!" she yelled –ABabu knew she was frightened of frogs. A neighbor, Asku appeared: "Anybody home?" All of them exploded into laughter. "Look, Emma," ABabu still held the frog up to his mother.

She ignored him. "OH! A cat from the neighborhood has snuck into the house and spilled all the milk? "The milk stored in the pot next to the fireplace was in a puddle. ABabu let go of the frog. "If I see that cat, I will beat her." Negate said.

"If you beat her, she won't give us back our milk," ABabu laughed. "Yes, that is true, but she will never do it again, so she will learn a lesson out of it." Negate answered lovingly.

"Will you beat me, too, if I bring back the frog?" ABabu bit his finger and left the room. "I know you won't do it again!" Negate shouted after him.

ABabu run to Negate and held her close.

Emma, I love you." "I love you too," she said, kissing his forehead.

In the village, children carried messages between homes; there were no telephones, electricity, or running water. One morning Negate sent ABabu to her neighbor, Asku. "Please tell Asku to come and have coffee," she asked him.

"Okay, if you give me sugar cane."

"Yes," she told him. "I will buy you some when I go to the marketplace." ABabu rubbed his head, running out the door. He returned back: "What was the message?"

"You didn't give attention to the message, ABabu! Listening is very important."

Habitu's voice rang in their ears; he was back from his farm chores. "You came early; are you okay?" Negate was surprised to see him. "I couldn't plow any longer; one of the oxen is not feeling good," he replied.

Negate offered him a water bucket to wash his feet and hands; once he was clean, she then offered him *injera* and *watt* (Ethiopian bread, made from the grain *teff*, and Ethiopian stew). They loved and respected one another; they cared as well for their animals, providing shelter and nursing them when they could.

Habitu was worried for the sick ox; the village had no veterinarian.

"Listen, Habitu – give him salt and pepper with water," Negate suggested. "Okay, you are right – that will help him. "The next morning, the sick ox was indeed better and deployed to his regular duty, plowing not just for Habitu but also for other farmers in turn, according to the village custom.

This custom provided sufficient food for the villagers – they had corn, barley, maize and wheat; in the hot season, they grew the best coffee in the region. Good Hope villagers also grew fruit: bananas, mangoes, lemons, papayas, blueberries, blackberries, and cranberries; and vegetables: carrots, cabbages, pumpkins, and potatoes. ABabu helped his mother in the garden, and would ask for carrots to much until the meal was ready.

All the farmers and their families helped in spring – with the promise of growth and fertility for the year – and at harvest time, the proof of achievement. On free days they would get together for festivals, and the villagers showed gratitude to nature – the young ones in dance and song, and the old ones in prayer. The girls and boys would dress in white robes, the girls braiding and tied their hair with black ribbon and the boys combing their Afros with wooden combs. ABabu loved to imitate the older boys.

Harvest brought *Buhe,* a special celebration for the village boys; they would go from house to house singing *Buhe Mata Ya Melata, Keba Kebute Indynata ("That bald Buha is here; anoint him with butter to make him look oily").* And getting presents in return for their efforts.

That is, until the fertile land was fertile no more – stricken by drought, the area became famous for its famine; not only the humans who were hungry, the air, the sky, the ground and rivers too. Nature slammed its door....

The youngsters respected their elders, and thereby won respect in return from their elders. Through this respect, the children behaved themselves, and the villagers lived in harmony, respecting the laws of man and God. This way, the village was crime-free.

The villagers have unique characteristics whether they are acquainted or not when they meet on pathways greeting each other is inevitable. At the same time they made inquiries, "What is news?"

Saturday was market day for Good Hope villagers – a free day to take a break from exhausting farm chores. Families brought their produce to exchange at the market for salt, kerosene, and special holiday clothing. On rare occasions, they splurged on soap; normally though, they used *endod,* the plant widely used in the countryside for washing clothes. After they made their purchases, boys and girls played together before returning to Good Hope – throwing lemons or solarium fruit to one another, signifying "I love you.

ABabu went to market with his parents, Negate riding the mule and Habitu riding along with ABabu behind him, astride a horse. Habitu had been a tenant farmer all his life. The landlord at Good Hope kept his peasants busy; men and women labored together, carrying their children upon their backs between the narrow, paved paths around the land, allowing the donkeys and mules passage.

Habitu worked from a young age, dawn to sunset, dreaming of his own farm. Even when crops failed, he did not give up. Then, when he was grown, after struggling for so long, his dream was fulfilled; later the word came to Good Hope; 'Land for the Peasants.' Good Hope villagers were allowed to own land at last, and ABabu's parents gained a plot of land to call their own. Upon attaining this goal, they next dreamed of literacy: Habitu saw his son, ABabu, in the city, attaining an education.

Negate, for herself, worked a nearby farm whenever she could find the time. With no modern farming machinery, this work had to be done by hand.

One day ABabu asked his Grandma Tetna: "How did Mom and Dad happen to come together?"

"ABabu," she replied, "I think you should know by now that it is customary, among youngsters, to play the lemon-throwing game."

"Oh yes," ABabu interrupted. "Sorry, please go on."

"On the Saturday your parents met, Habitu saw Negate, a tall, thin girl, and decided she would be his future wife." ABabu relished the scene in his mind.

Grandma Tetna continued: "Habitu, your dad, consulted his friend Degu, mentioning her by name. Degu responded favorably."

"Habitu, if Negate is the one you are asking about, 'Degu told Habitu, 'she is an exceptionally good girl, and well liked by the neighborhood.' Degu stood up from his stool and affirmed Negate's character for Habitu. 'Don't miss your opportunity.' Degu told Habitu. 'In fact, I heard that a couple of other people from Lemlem Village were asking if she was already spoken for.' Habitu thought about this. Then he and Degu agreed to go to the village elders to ask for Negate's hand that next Sunday – of course, with the village elders' approval of the match."

Grandma Tetna continued her story: "Negate didn't know, that Sunday, who the elders were when they came to her door. She greeted them politely, offering them a mud bench for a seat near
the door, until we came back from church – quite a distance from Lemlem village.

"It was a pleasant morning with a hazy sky, fresh with tree scent and a soft bird song, refreshing mind and soul. As soon as we got home we knew that elders were there with a plan for Negate, and so we sent her to a relative's home with a message.

"The date was fixed for their marriage; Habitu didn't have much money for the wedding celebration, but that didn't worry us much at all. All his effort was aimed at getting a girl he loved at first sight. And that was how Negate and Habitu happened to get married." Grandma Tetna concluded. ABabu exploded with laughter, and kissed his grandma to thank her for the story.

Part Two: ABabu Grows

Adjacent to Good Hope Village there is a big forest, *Agudora*, home to many oak, cedar, koso, sycamore and olive trees, as well as many wild animals.

"Can you take me to the forest?" ABabu asked Habitu.

"Sure, when you grow older," Habitu told his son.

"What are wild animals?" ABabu asked.

"Wild animals are those who live far from the village, like lions, elephants, gorillas, tigers, antelopes, giraffes, leopards, hyenas, and cheetahs," Habitu explained.

"Aw! I want to see them!"

"When you get big like me," Habitu patiently told his son, "you will go and see them. These animals are dangerous; you need to be able to run fast to escape from them, or else you will have to be a hunter like Master Goabaz, our ex-landlord."

ABabu paused. "I will ask *Ababa* Goabaz when he comes."

"Yes, you could; but he will tell you that you are too young."

"Why does Master Goabaz wear an earring?" ABabu asked presently, "Can I have one?"

Both laughed; Habitu explained to ABabu, "Master Goabaz wears a pierced earring on his left ear; it's a sign that he is a great hunter."

"How long will it take me to grow?" ABabu and his father laughed again. Negate told him, "Next year, you will go to school and learn your alphabet, and read books; then you will learn a lot more about animals."

ABabu became experienced with the domestic animals on his parents' land: horses, mules, cows, oxen, goats, sheep, and hens. His best friend of all, however, was a *Korea* Dog. The family never bought eggs; they got them from their chicken. Negate would collect the eggs in a straw basket to use them for *doro watt*, a delicious chicken stew made with hard-boiled eggs. Early in the morning, and then again late in the evening Negate would milk the cows, letting ABabu get his share of fresh milk in his cup.

ABabu asked his parents for permission to go with his friends on *Buhe*'s day. Both Negate and Habitu agreed, warning him to be careful and return home early.

He complied; later on, he asked Negate if he could go outside to play.

"It is late, now," she told him.

"Okay. Can we ask riddles, then?"

All agreed to this... "A little blade will shave a land," ABabu proposed to the family. Habitu and Negate smiled and rambled a little, to guess the answer. Finally, Habitu came with an answer: "Fire?"

"Correct, correct!" ABabu out loud.

ABabu proposed another riddle.

"A Journey which has no end," Negate and Habitu puzzled for a while and Negate answered: "Thinking."

"Good answer, Mommy!" ABabu jumped up and down at her cleverness.

Negate brought *dabo* (bread) with yogurt for ABabu and Habitu. ABabu loved to wash his hands before and after eating; both he and his father gave God gratitude in prayer for the meal, and for Negate who served them. The day ended pleasantly.

Part Three: ABabu's Early School Days

ABabu, eager to go to school, could barely wait for the time to come. Habitu prepared for ABabu's big day by buying him khaki shorts and a shirt, as well as canvas shoes. Negate, nine months pregnant, prepared ABabu's lunch for him to carry in a straw basket.

"What is inside, Mommy?" ABabu touched his mother's tummy.

"A sister or a brother for you is inside," she responded, and they laughed.

ABabu's school, A Road to Knowledge, had a teacher, Zega – known for his teaching ability, good advice, and discipline. Zega believed in a child's ability to respond well to learning the difference between good and bad at an early age. ABabu called him Teacher Zega. At playtime, ABabu would play hide and seek, and with mud and clay, with his friends. They did not need Mickey Mouse to entertain them; they enjoyed what was available. At the beginning of each day – until this day – the students sing the Ethiopian national anthem and fly its green, yellow, and red flag.

Under the shade of a tree, Teacher Zega would tell the students about the monkey and honey. "A smart monkey snuck to a farm and climbed a tree, snatching some honey from a hive. He tried to run away fast, but the bee owner heard the sound and, catching the monkey, pinched him on the ear. 'Never take someone's property without permission,' the farmer told the monkey.

"That monkey told the other monkeys not to go back to the farm." Teacher Zega reinforced the lesson to the students: "When you need something, ask your parents for it." ABabu and the other students agreed, clapping their hands.

When ABabu went home that evening, Negate bought him a bunch of sugar cane from the sugar cane seller. ABabu was delighted, and told his parents the monkey story. "It is a good story," both Habitu and Negate agreed.

ABabu finished the alphabet in forty days. "It is fun! I love to go to school! And when I grow up, I want to be a teacher!" Habitu and Negate admired his wish, encouraging him to study hard. ABabu is the class cheerleader.

One day ABabu came home with a new puzzle. "Ali lost a camel," he shared with his parents. "While searching for his camel, he met a man, asking him if he had seen such an animal."

"Yes, 'the stranger answered, 'I saw a one-eyed camel.'" ABabu continued with the puzzle: "Yes, that was the lost camel; where did you see it?' Ali asked the man. The stranger then replied, 'I didn't see it in reality, but I knew a lost camel must be one-eyed.' How would a stranger know Ali's camel was one-eyed?" ABabu posed.

Negate and Habitu laughed over the puzzle, and thought about it. Finally Habitu responded, "The stranger knew the camel was one-eyed because when a camel grazes, it doesn't graze on the blinded side. Unless your classmates come up with a better answer, you can share this answer with your teacher."

Part Four: The Birth of a New Baby

Negate, tall and beautiful, shortened her conversation with her neighbors and concentrated on her back pain. Neighbors were gathered to have coffee, but Negate had realized quickly she was in labor. She shortened the conversation and concentrated on her pain. She kneeled down on the deck near the fireplace.

"Has your water broken already?" one of the neighbors asked. "I think soon." Put more wood on the fire, and prepare some water and a blade," she demanded. It was almost mid-day; Negate sweated in the heat of the small room. "Come now, hold my back," she told Asku. "Do not try to sit straight; remain as you are; push hard," another neighbor encouraged.

The baby – soon to be named Mena – cleared her long passageway and arrived before long into the world. Negate was well prepared to be her own midwife – there was no one to serve as such in the village. Asku efficiently tied and cut off the umbilical cord, cleaning the newborn. The neighbors expressed their happiness, dancing and singing the *illilta.* Zena, Negate's friend, rushed to the kitchen to make *Genfo* – barley or wheat porridge – to build Negate's strength; the villagers believed that a woman, upon giving birth, should eat nutritious food or become weak and unhealthy the rest of her life. The neighbors shared the meal; the tradition in Ethiopian culture is that whatever you have, you share with family and friends.

"Get me some warm water; let me wash my breast and suckle her," Negate requested of Asku. "Negate!" Asku replied. "Give her a little fenugreek, too; that will help her digestion."

Soon Habitu appeared with a sheep to be slaughtered, as a treat for Negate. Friends and neighbors were ready with handmade clothes for the newborn girl.

ABabu was overjoyed to see his baby sister when he returned from school that day. He wanted to hold her, but everyone laughed and explained that she was still too small to be held. When ABabu saw the tiny clothes for her, he asked if he could dress Mena. Habitu and Negate promised him that he could dress her when she got a bit bigger.

They discussed their newborn daughter's future. Habitu believed in good housekeeping, and wished for baby Mena to become a good housekeeper, learning to cook, to mend, and to be obedient – and become an honest and loving mother like her mother and his wife, Negate. Negate, for her part, wished for Mena to have a good education, to be able to avoid an oppressive and abusive life, and to be economically self-sufficient.

"She will be a teacher, like her brother!" ABabu weighed in. Everyone smiled.

Part Five: The Move to Town

Negate and Habitu decided to move to town, to provide a better education for ABabu and Mena. They were lost in a jungle of thoughts. "I have no complaints," Habitu said. "Things will be better for our children when they get an education. It is an important aspect in life, and our children should not have to repeat the life we have had. Let us move forward." When ABabu heard the news, he was overjoyed – except for the thought of leaving his best friend, *Korea* Dog, and their other animals behind.

The family packed their belongings, selling a few of their goats, sheep, one cow and oxen. Korea Dog, though, was considered part of the family; they couldn't leave their best friend behind. So ABabu, Mena, *Korea* Dog, Habitu and Negate traveled to Rainbow Town on foot.

It was pleasant listening to the birds twittering, and watching herds graze in the pastures, climbing the mountain and crossing the valley, smelling different natural aromas, and admiring nature.

Their first encounter on the road was an elephant. "Who is this?" ABabu, surprised, turned his face to his dad.

"This is an elephant," Habitu whispered to his son.

ABabu smiled and approached the elephant, touching his ear. The elephant, in turn, sniffed him and flapped his big ear. It then offered ABabu and his family a ride to a nearby village, where they could spend the night, gesturing 'Happy journey' as it left them. ABabu was thrilled with the friendly and unique care of the elephant, calling him 'Uncle.'

The second day of their journey, they met up with a lion. Again, ABabu asked his father, "Who is this?"

"This is a lion," Habitu whispered fearfully. "He is called king of the jungle."

"Can I go close to him and touch his soft hair?"

"No," Habitu murmured. "No, you stay where you are." The lion moved gracefully, peacefully on to his forest. The family was thankful at his peaceful departure; afterward they rested under shade trees, and ate the food they carried in their straw baskets, and drank the water from their gourds. Finally they continued their journey.

On the third day, as they approached Rainbow Town, they met a hyena. This most unpleasant creature nearly scared them all to death; Korea Dog was ready to pounce on it. "Who is this, Dad?" ABabu screamed. Habitu held ABabu's hand and, calming him, replied, "This is hyena." ABabu calmed down at the familiar name.

At each village stop, the family was treated hospitably, kindly. After three days of adventure, they finally arrived at Rainbow Town. Their house had rough curved walls, painted with white lime. A small window was cut into stone; the floors were slate. Colorful hand-woven baskets hung on the wall, and small cushions decorated the floor. It was tidy and clean. Negate's sister, Fikere, was prepared to meet her family with whatever things could afford; she had heard some time before the message that her sister and family was coming. Though Fikere did not have *tefe injera,* the special bread privileged people eat; she brought plenty of fruit and corn pies with milk.

Preparing a sleeping place for ABabu and his parents, Fikere soaked and washed her bed sheets. She offered *Korea* Dog corn bread and water. Though she had a limited income, she provided the best hospitality she could offer.

Fikere had lived for many years in Rainbow Town, and spoke fast, like a native Adera – considered talkative. Fikere, too, preferred to talk rather than to listen. She took some coffee beans from the token bundle her sister had brought. She made coffee, and offered fresh milk to ABabu and Mena; she sprinkled grass, and the smoke of the incense circulating in that small room looked like a cloud without destination. The room smelled delicious; Negate and Habitu thanked Fikere for her kindness and hospitality.

While ABabu and Mena slept, Fikere and Negate shared childhood memories. They had played with mud and rocks, chasing one another around the cottages. They had picked solarium fruit and thrown it to each other, mimicking the bigger boys and girls expressing their 'I love you."

As they went on, Negate asked: "I do not recall a single instance of child abuse in our home. Do you, Fikere?"

"Yes—there was one thing that bothered me: the old way – done indiscriminately to boys and girls." Fikere was ashamed to say it out loud. Negate knew what she meant, and both agreed that educating the people would play a great role in stopping the abuse of circumcision for future generations. They expressed their painful memories to one another.

"In our family, we like to share; when there is plenty of everything," Negate stated, "people are greedy."

"Fifty lemons to carry is a load for one person," Fikere quoted the proverb: "one lemon per person is aroma." Habitu patted Fikere with a genuine smile on his face. Fikere adored ABabu and Mena for their educational ambitions.

Fikere was a widow who had no children of her own, but dearly loved her nephew ABabu and niece Mena. The majority of Good Hope villagers subscribed to the belief, "No point to worry about tomorrow." She expressed this to her sister and brother-in-law.

"Yes, we all lived this way, "Habitu replied, "except for the landlords who owned land from edge to edge. Now this is a new era; we worry for our children's future – if they can be educated and work hard, they can have a bright future."

Fikere was never alone; one of her neighbors – Kedija, an Adera woman - greeted her in her native language: "*Amman Aderish*? (Good morning?)" Fikere assured her that she was heard, and the woman glanced through Fikere's half-open door to determine whether Fikere was alone. Fikere greeted her in return, asked her if she would come in. Kedija rushed in with a hand-woven basket to take to *meghalla* – or market – so as not to miss the early morning shopping.

ABabu was excited by the new experience, and attended to his surroundings. Another friend, Fatoum, appeared, knocking on the door, carrying milk in a hollowed-out pumpkin on her head. "*Amman Aderish*!" Fatoum wore a colorful, attractive costume; she spoke quickly, the Adera custom. "*Amman Aderish,*" Fikere replied.

"Do you buy milk?" Fatoum offered. (Milk is being carried with goured for sale house to house.)

"I already bought," Fikere replied.

Negate and Habitu reminded themselves that this was the lifestyle accustomed in Good Hope Village.

Part Six: School in Rainbow Town and Beyond

ABabu began his second educational phase in his new school, "Morning Star," with his new teacher, Hagar. Opposite the school he found a hyena house with many different colorful flags aloft.

"What is that flag for?" ABabu asked Teacher Hagar; he had only noticed the flag, not the purpose of the building.

"That is the hyenas' empire," responded Teacher Hagar. "They live there with a man who feeds them with meat and bones. That is for the attraction of tourists."

"What is a tourist?" ABabu asked.

"Tourists are those people who come to know and learn of new things, from near or far places. There are people who come from faraway countries, especially *Ferinji*."

"What is *Ferinji*?" ABabu was curious.

"Ferinji are white people, or Westerners, who come from very far places to see what they don't see in their own country. *Ferinji* are supposed to be educated; they are those who went to the moon."

ABabu was surprised at this, and became lost in thought. He had not seen any other color of people than the Arabian incense merchant, who sold incense from house to house. "If you become a very brave student," Teacher Hagar continued, "you will have a chance to go to *Ferinji* country to advance your education."

ABabu returned home with his new friend, Tutu. He carried a letter for his family:

"Mom and Dad, you should be proud of me.

Now, I can read a big book.

Soon, I will go to a country called Ferinji country.

Habitu and Negate were pleased with ABabu's progress; but Habitu took his hand and gave ABabu a piece of advice. "First, we all need to know our own country well. If we go back to our country's history of war with Italy, we see that a lack of preparation and modern machinery not allowed the Italians to invade our country.

Our country's solidarity and unity put the Italians on the defensive, and drove them out of our country for good. We are proud of our country and we should resemble our forbears and their heroism. Our color is our beauty and our identity.

"This is what I learned from my father, son, and I am passing this short message on to you."

***

ABabu made a kite of paper, incense wax, and string after school, to play with his friend Tutu. He had great enthusiasm for all his subjects, and got a prize from the principal for being the best student at school. His family admired his talent.

ABabu loved to listen to jokes. One time he brought home the following joke from school:

There was a prince and a princess who lived in a place called Peace Land. One day the princess went to the Royal Prince's Office and knocked on his door.

"Who is that?" The prince asked.

"Princess of Peace Land," the princess answered. The prince did not open his door.

Again, the princess knocked. With a loud voice, the prince asked again: "Who is that?"

"Princess Amber." Still, she got no response from the prince. For the third time, Princess knocked again. The Prince awoke with a louder voice still: "Who is that!"

This time, the princess, in a low voice, answered. "This is your wife." Finally, the prince opened the door for his wife, Princess. Amber.

The family exploded into laughter.

***

ABabu, eager to accomplish his goal, and make his wish come true, completed his education and went back to Good Hope Village eventually to teach. His ambition was to eradicate illiteracy from the village. "One day," he joked, "we might land on the moon."

Would you like to see your manuscript become a book?

If you are interested in becoming a PublishAmerica author, please submit your manuscript for possible publication to us at:

acquisitions@publishamerica.com

You may also mail in your manuscript to:

**PublishAmerica
PO Box 151
Frederick, MD 21705**

www.publishamerica.com

Breinigsville, PA USA
11 April 2011
259600BV00002B/59/P